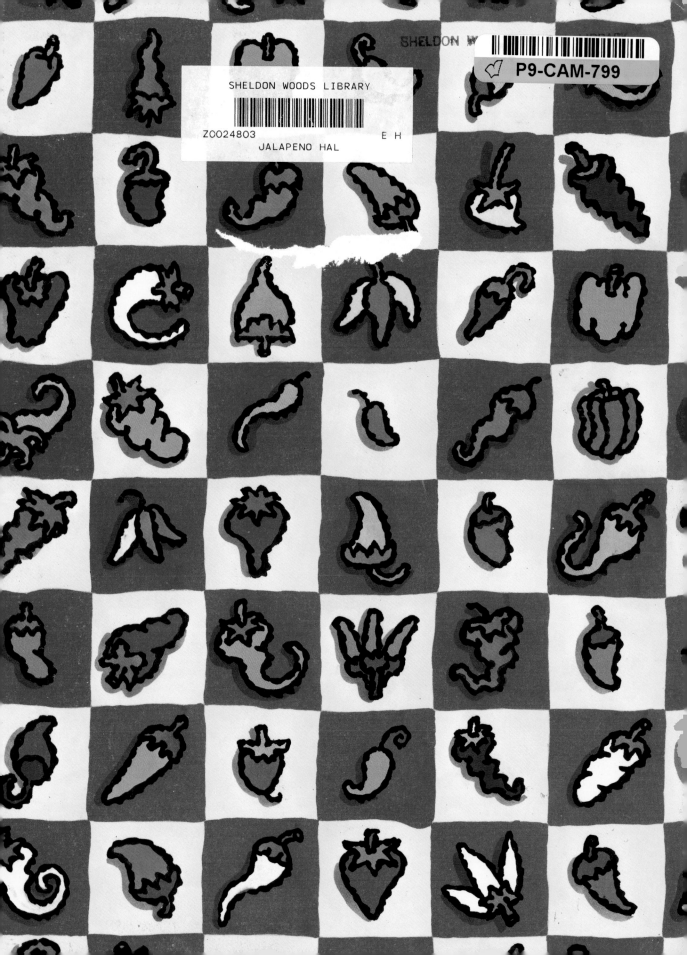

Jalapeño Hal

Four Winds Press ☀ New York

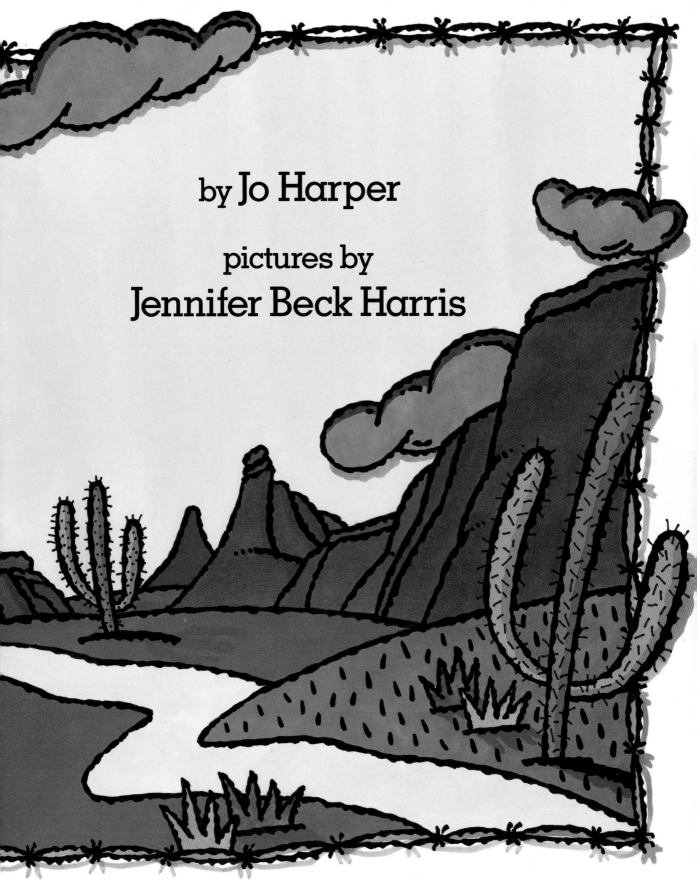

by Jo Harper

pictures by
Jennifer Beck Harris

Maxwell Macmillan Canada   Toronto   Maxwell Macmillan International   New York   Oxford   Singapore   Sydney

A NOTE TO READERS
Picante often means hot and spicy flavoring.
Picante is also a hot sauce made with tomatoes,
onions, peppers, vinegar, and other condiments.

Macmillan Publishing Company is part of
the Maxwell Communication Group of Companies.

Four Winds Press
Macmillan Publishing Company
866 Third Avenue
New York, NY 10022

Maxwell Macmillan Canada, Inc.
1200 Eglinton Avenue East
Suite 200
Don Mills, Ontario M3C 3N1

First edition
Printed and bound in Hong Kong by South China Printing Co. (1988) Ltd.
10 9 8 7 6 5 4 3 2 1
The text of this book is set in Nashville Medium.
The illustrations are rendered in ink and dyes.
Book design by Christy Hale

Library of Congress Cataloging-in-Publication Data
Harper, Jo.
Jalapeño Hal / Jo Harper; pictures by Jennifer Beck Harris—1st ed.
p. cm.
Summary: Rough and tough Jalapeño Hal finds a way
to bring rain to a dry Texas town.
ISBN 0-02-742645-9
[1. Cowboys—Fiction. 2. Peppers—Fiction. 3. Texas—Fiction.]
I. Harris, Jennifer Beck, date. ill. II. Title.
PZ7.H23135Jal 1993
[E]—dc20 92-16921

To De Aaon, who sang the tale's tune

—J.H.

He may not wear boots
or a ten-gallon hat,
but no other Texan was ever tougher.
To Roger

—J.B.H.

Jalapeño Hal was a rough, tough cowboy. He was tough as a boot. He was tough as nails. He was tough as a horned toad's hide in summer. His heart was made of stone, and he was proud of it.

Jalapeño Hal rode a red mustang named Cayenne. They roamed in Big Bend, the roughest part of Texas. But they didn't wander down by the Rio Grande, where there was water, because every few days a boatload of people would go by, making noise. That irritated Hal. Out where Hal roamed, the only sound was his own lonesome song....

> Give me a chili pepper,
> A jalapeño pepper.
> Toss me a little hot pepper.
> Picante is what I need!

eople used to wonder how Hal could live in that bone-dry country where there wasn't water—just coyotes, and mountain lions, and rattlesnakes. But Hal didn't care. He was mean and he had mean breath...scorching-hot breath. This was because Jalapeño Hal ate so many jalapeño peppers.

If he frowned at a coyote, that coyote would slink away. If he blew his hot jalapeño breath at a mountain lion, that lion would leap over boulders to get back up a mountain. And Hal ate the rattlesnakes—in rattlesnake stew.

ometimes Hal *had* to go to town. Sometimes he needed a lariat, or a new pair of boots, or a new Stetson hat. When that happened he went to Presidio, but being so close to people made Hal scowl.

Jalapeño Hal was a rough, tough cowboy, and the folks in Presidio were scared of him. Murveen Manning's fat, happy baby, Essie Mae, started crying whenever Hal walked by. Billy Bob Barker and Fanny Faye Cox hid behind their mamas' skirts. Strong Sheriff Hawkins shook in his boots. Even Buck Garret, the burly blacksmith, trembled and turned pale. And the meanest dog in town, Old Bravo, whimpered and hid.

ut there was one person in Presidio who wasn't scared—a boy. This boy lived with his mama, Sadie. She was a widow woman, and they lived in a tidy little house with flowers all around it. Sadie had named her son Christopher, and she wanted him to be kind and gentle. Christopher called himself Kit. He wanted to be tough.

When Jalapeño Hal rode into Presidio, Kit gave Cayenne a cookie. When Hal rode down the street, Kit followed, riding tough and eating jalapeño peppers just like his hero. Hal never scowled at Kit.

hen Sadie saw Kit following Jalapeño Hal, she felt nervous. When Kit came home, she scolded. ''Christopher, you worry me completely crazy! Jalapeño Hal is too rough and tough! Go brush your teeth! You have horrible jalapeño breath!''

But Sadie didn't need to worry. Hal never stayed in Presidio long. He always rode away into the sunset. And when he did, Kit missed him. Time passed. Every day as Kit rode his new pony, Pepper, he kept looking toward the horizon, hoping to see his hero coming.

Then a terrible thing happened in Presidio.
It didn't rain for a long time, and the wells dried
up. Sadie's flowers died. The grass turned
brown. The trees began to wither. Nobody could
take a bath. Dust blew in the streets.

Horses quit whinnying. Cows didn't moo. The meanest dog in town, Old Bravo, quit growling. Finally folks couldn't talk to each other anymore, because their throats were so dry. The whole town of Presidio was silent.

Something had to be done, and Kit knew what it was. He mounted Pepper and headed for Big Bend. It was a long, hot, thirsty ride, but Kit found Hal—leaning against a cactus, cooking rattlesnake stew.

Kit cleared his throat, and in a dry, raspy voice, he told Hal of the trouble in Presidio. ''We need . . . the help . . . of a tough hombre,'' he said.

Hal narrowed his eyes, tipped his head back against the cactus, and thought. He could feel his stone heart cold against his ribs.

Then Hal looked Kit straight in the eyes.
''I'm the toughest hombre in Texas,'' he said.
''I'm the man for the job.''

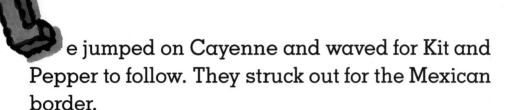

e jumped on Cayenne and waved for Kit and Pepper to follow. They struck out for the Mexican border.

When they got to the Rio Grande, Kit thought they would fill some barrels and carry water back to Presidio. But they didn't. They just paused long enough for Kit to wet his whistle. Then, riding past rocks and cactus, they headed on into Mexico.

And as the two tough cowboys rode across the desert, Hal taught Kit this song....

Give me a chili pepper,
A jalapeño pepper.
Toss me a little hot pepper.
Picante is what I need!

Hal and Kit kept going until they came to a big field of peppers. Then they jumped off their horses and started picking as fast as they could. They picked baskets of jalapeño peppers.

They picked sacks of chili peppers. They filled
their hats with peppers. They started back to
Presidio loaded down with peppers.

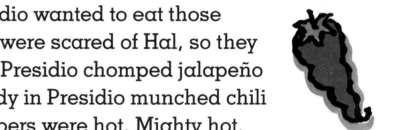

en they arrived, Hal and Kit started handing out peppers. They gave them to Sheriff Hawkins, to Billy Bob Barker, to Fanny Faye Cox, and to Murveen Manning. They even gave them to baby Essie Mae, and they gave a hatful to burly Buck Garret. And of course, they gave them to Sadie. Then they gave peppers to the horses, the cows, and the dogs.

''EAT 'EM!'' Hal said, and scowled.

Nobody in Presidio wanted to eat those peppers. But they were scared of Hal, so they did. Everybody in Presidio chomped jalapeño peppers. Everybody in Presidio munched chili peppers. The peppers were hot. Mighty hot.

''EAT MORE!'' Jalapeño Hal yelled.

Folks' noses stung. Their eyes watered. And their tongues were on fire. But when Hal yelled, everyone in Presidio trembled and crammed their mouths full.

''CHEW FASTER!'' Hal bellowed.

Sheriff Hawkins chewed faster. Buck Garret chomped. So did Billy Bob and Fanny Faye. Even Essie Mae crunched more and more peppers. The dogs, cows, and horses gobbled faster and faster.

And then steam started coming out of their
ears. Steam started coming out of their noses.
Soon the whole town of Presidio was covered
with steam.

he steam got thicker and thicker, like a heavy fog. The fog gathered into a cloud and rose into the air. Lightning flashed. Thunder rolled. All the folk in Presidio stopped chewing, looked up into the sky, and grinned. They hadn't seen a storm in a long, long time.

Rain began to fall. It fell on the dry flower beds. It fell on the brown grass. It fell on the wilted trees. It filled the horse troughs, the cow tanks, and the dog bowls. It filled the city lake. The folks in Presidio tipped back their heads, opened their grinning mouths, and let the raindrops run down their burning, dry throats.

Soon children were splashing in puddles.
Cows mooed. Horses whinnied. Old Bravo
frolicked like a puppy. Folks lifted Hal and Kit up
onto their shoulders and marched around the
town square. They yelled, ''Yippee for Kit!''
Then they yelled, ''Hooray for Jalapeño Hal!''

Right then Jalapeño Hal decided that some sounds were nice to hear. He decided that sometimes it was fun to be around people. And as soon as he decided that, he felt his stone heart melt and turn into Jell-O. . . .

These days Hal doesn't live all alone in Big Bend. He didn't *tell* anybody that his heart had gone soft, but nobody was scared of him anymore. They elected him mayor of Presidio. He keeps jalapeño peppers in the town hall for emergencies.

These days Sadie thinks Hal is pretty good company. Now that she eats jalapeño peppers, too, she doesn't mind his hot breath. Hal, Sadie, and Kit often walk to the edge of town to watch the sun set over the mountains.

But Hal is still tough. Tough as a nail. Tough
as a boot. Tough as a horned toad's hide in
winter. And so is Kit. Sometimes Hal and Kit
get to feeling cramped. Then they saddle up
Cayenne and Pepper and head for Big Bend,
where there are wide open spaces and plenty
of quiet.

They don't mind the coyotes and mountain
lions, they eat the rattlesnakes, and they've
been known to sing as they roam...

Give me a chili pepper,
A jalapeño pepper.
Toss me a little hot pepper.
Picante is what I need!

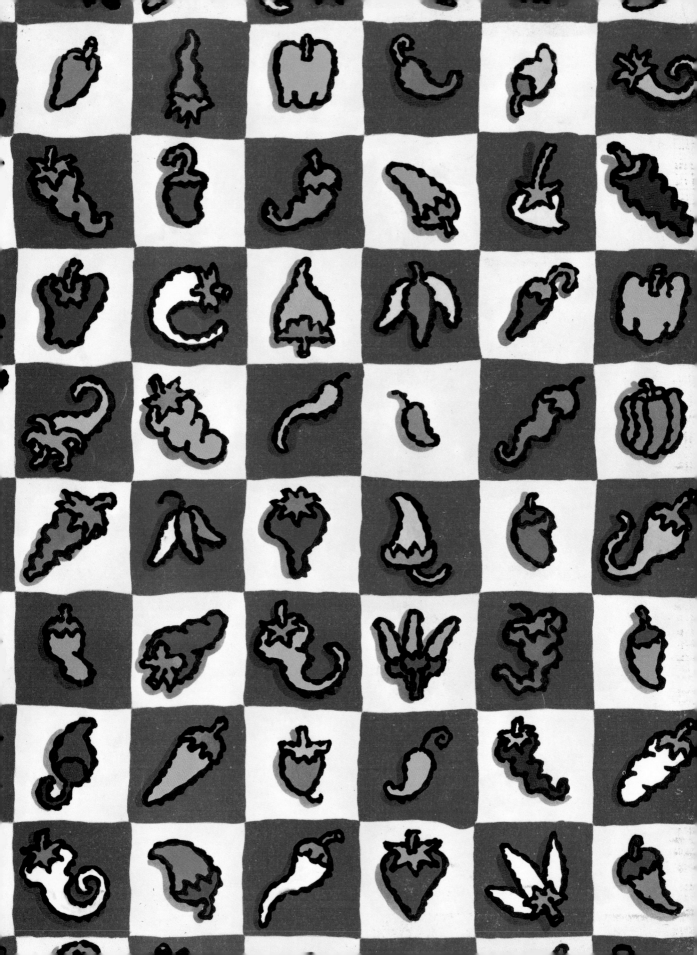